To Mary Oliver: I hope to be your
keeper of wild words. —B. S.

For my parents. —M. K.

Library of Congress Cataloging-in-Publication Data available.

ISBN 978-1-4521-7073-2

Manufactured in China.

FSC
www.fsc.org
MIX
Paper from
responsible sources
FSC™ C008047

Design by Jennifer Tolo Pierce.
Typeset in Poynter and Naive Sans.
The illustrations in this book were rendered in mixed media and Photoshop.

10 9 8 7 6 5 4 3

Chronicle Books LLC
680 Second Street
San Francisco, California 94107

Chronicle Books—we see things differently. Become part
of our community at www.chroniclekids.com.

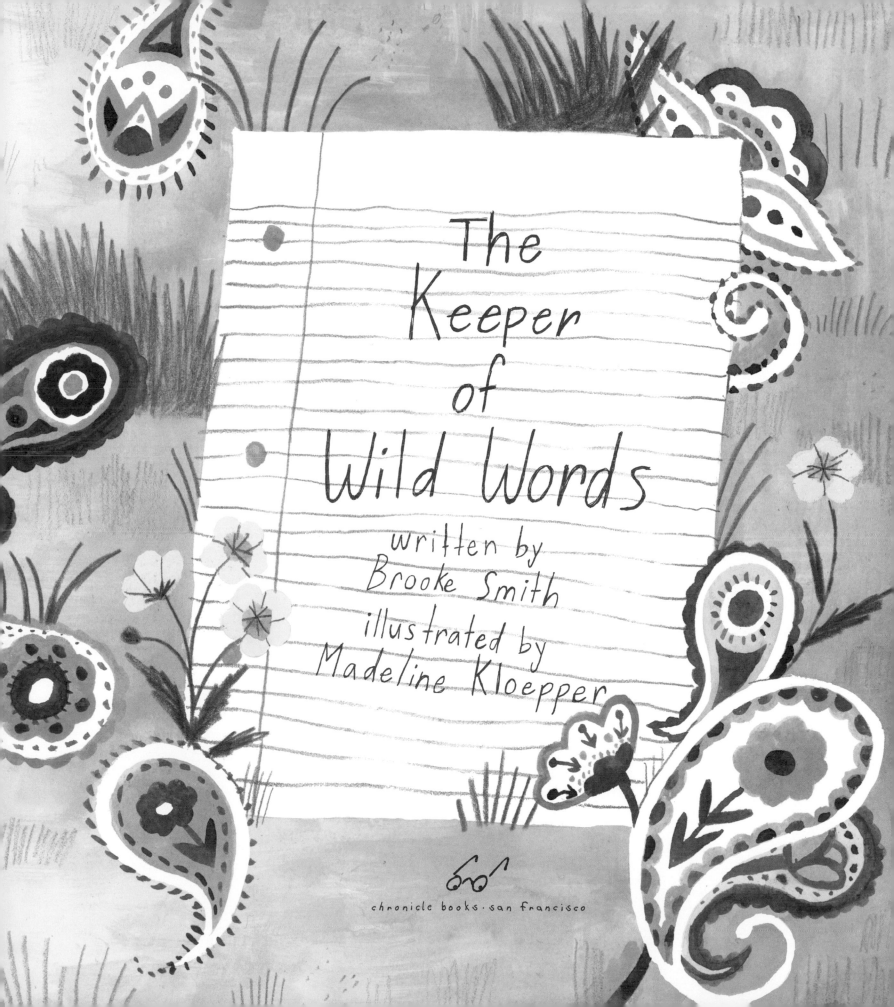

The Keeper of Wild Words

written by
Brooke Smith

illustrated by
Madeline Kloepper

chronicle books·san francisco

At the end of a long cinder lane,
surrounded by meadows
and pine trees and sky
that wrapped around and back again,

Brook ran up to her grandmother's door,
swung it open,
and she belonged.

"Mimi, I'm here!"

Brook called her grandmother Mimi.
She wasn't just a grandmother,
she was a grand friend.

Mimi had been waiting.
She'd been sitting at her desk all day,
distracted by a hummingbird,
a wasp's nest,
a red-tailed hawk hovering overhead.

Mimi was a writer.
She wove words into everything,
everything that mattered.

Brook was so excited to be visiting.
She needed Mimi's help.
Tomorrow was the first day of school,
and Brook had nothing for show and tell.

Her summer had been wonderful,
but she didn't have one special thing to share
that her friends would always remember.

But today, Mimi needed Brook's help, too.
She had something important to ask her.

"I'm afraid some of my favorite words are disappearing.

Some of the wild words that I've known and loved my whole life."

"How do words disappear?"
Brook wondered.

"Words disappear if we don't share
them when we talk.
If we don't write them in our stories.
If we don't read them in our books."

"If we don't use words, they can be forgotten.

And if they're forgotten . . .
they disappear."

"I need someone to keep them safe,"
she continued.
"To help remember. I need you to be my Keeper . . .

The Keeper of Wild Words."

"Can I wear a crown?" Brook asked.

"No," Mimi laughed, "the Keeper doesn't need a crown.
She just needs to keep her eyes wide open,
and be ready to see and hear and feel all the wild words.
That way, she'll always remember them."

"Look."

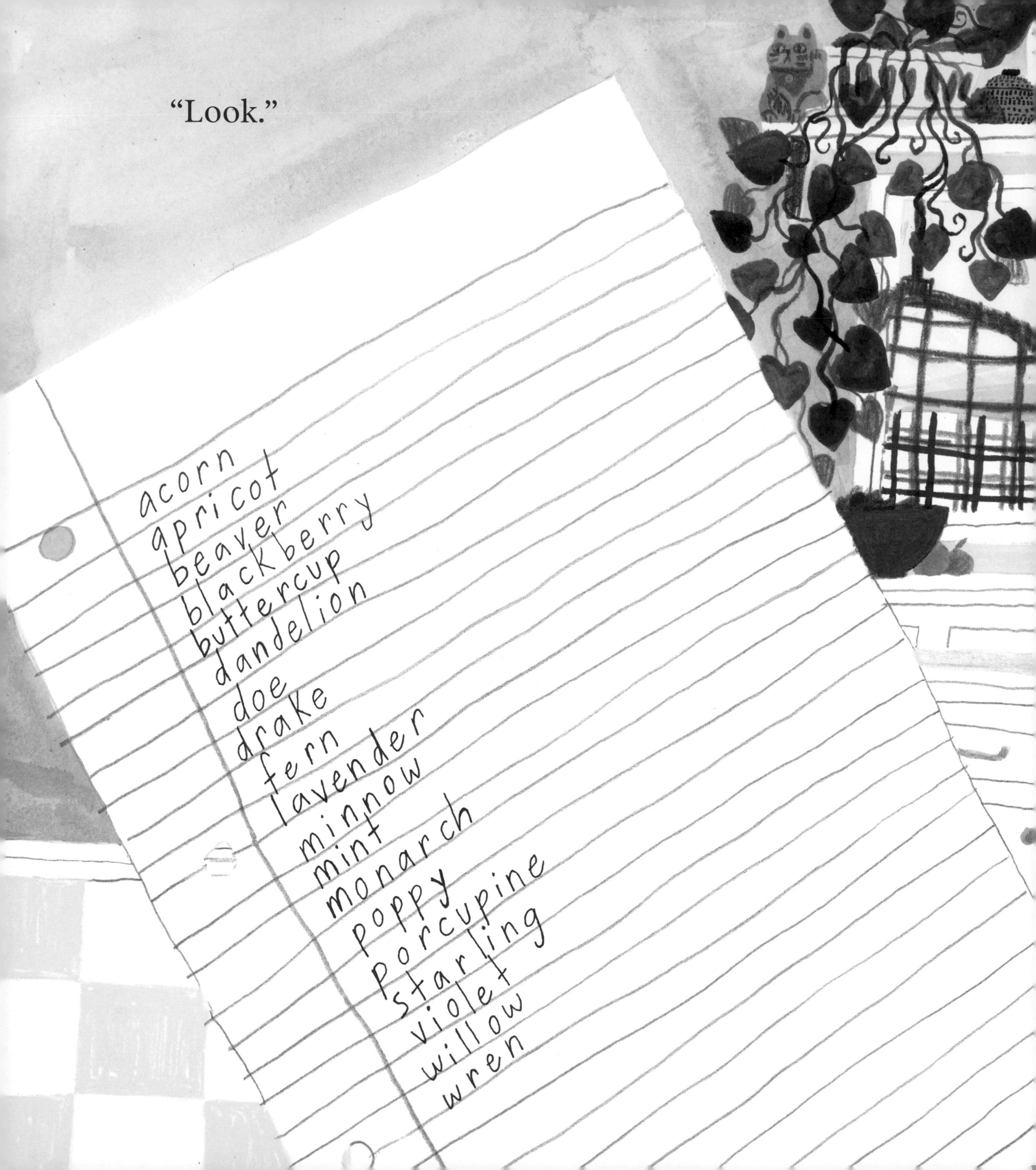

acorn
apricot
beaver
blackberry
buttercup
dandelion
doe
drake
fern
lavender
minnow
mint
monarch
poppy
porcupine
starling
violet
willow
wren

"From sunup to sundown,
   we'll walk and run and walk again,
   sit and wait,
   listen and touch,
   until we find every word on
   the list," said Mimi.
   "Or every word on the list finds us."

"I'm ready," said Brook, and they were off.
And sure enough,
as soon as they stepped into the morning,
wild words were waiting . . .

A WREN sang a good morning song,
a little brown bird with a voice like an angel.
Sitting up high, looking down
just waiting to say hello to the world.

Bunches of VIOLETS spread underfoot.
Sweet perfume filled the air, almost making
Brook dizzy.
Their little purple faces smiled,
inviting the day to begin.

POPPIES in the corner of the yard
suddenly popped open!
Paper petals reaching to the sun.

And bushes filled with BLACKBERRIES
just like the ones Brook had eaten for breakfast.
Hundreds still waiting to be picked
and enjoyed for dessert.

Do wild words dance like this
every morning?

Along the way, Brook picked up an ACORN
that fell from a mighty oak.
Big towering oak tree,
little nut with a tiny brown hat, smooth round shell.
She put it in her pocket, to remember.

Up ahead they saw light,
reflected in a round mirror of water . . .

the pond!

When Brook scooped up a handful of water,
silver MINNOWS swam circles
in her palm, now a pool.
Whoever knew she could hold the wild?

Then splash!
Silence broken. A BEAVER jumped in
and then under he went,
swimming towards his den,
climbing up on the other side of the pond,
and then disappearing from view.

"It's surc busy around here!" Brook said.
"Always," Mimi answered.

Bushels of MINT surrounded the pond.
Mimi picked stems and rubbed the leaves
in her fingers.
Brook picked a leaf and put it in her mouth.

Fresh!
Sweet!
Tangy!

From the ground.
From the earth.
She could taste the wild.

Then one last visitor waddled by.
Green-velvet head, bright-yellow beak.
Mr. DRAKE, papa duck running.
Quack! Run!

Lift off! Wings out . . .

There he goes!

Where next? The meadow!
Just follow the trail,
cut deep in the tall grass.

Brook ran ahead.
So free! So free! So free!

A butterfly, a MONARCH,
diving in the breeze.
"Now you are just like me!"

Bright BUTTERCUPS welcomed them,
yellow petals glistening in the sun.
A wild carpet of light and beauty.

"Quick! Make a wish!" said Mimi,
holding out a DANDELION,
fairy dust sitting on a stem.

"Blow on it and the seeds will fly.
Your tiny wishes in the air."

At the top of the meadow stood an old WILLOW tree.
The shade of the willow was like a dear friend.
Mimi had known this tree forever.

"What a perfect place to have lunch," Mimi said.
She took out small sandwiches
and APRICOTS, picked from her yard.
Round, fuzzy fruit, sweet as could be,
the juice dripping with every bite.

Rows of LAVENDER lined the field below,
filling the air with a magic perfume.

Just then, overhead—
Brook could not believe her eyes!
"There's a bird cloud flying above us!"

"Oh my!" Mimi said, "the STARLINGS are back!
Such an amazing wonder."

Thousands of birds swooped, darted,
and turned, somehow always staying connected.
Then they floated away, as mysteriously as they came.

Finally they wandered over to the dense, dark woods.
Brook had always been a little afraid of the forest,
but now part of her was wild,
and she couldn't wait.

A light rain started to fall,
sudden summer shower.
The rain made the smells of the forest come alive
and all the plants glisten.

The FERNS with their magnificent, green-feathered leaves
curled up and then spread out like a fan
for everyone to notice.

"What else do you see?" Mimi asked.
Brook looked across the forest floor
and sure enough, nestled in the needles,
was a DOE, a deer
curled up like the fern,
fast asleep in the shadows.

"Quiet.
Quiet.
Peace and quiet.
Walk slowly by, we'll let her be."

In the woods things appear
around corners, tucked deep.
Ahead they heard a rustling.

"Stop!" Mimi said. "Walk back
slowly towards me."

Right then, a PORCUPINE
popped out and ran up a tree!
Porcupines, if they're scared, will let their quills fly.

Surprises abound in the wild.

Mimi had one other surprise.
"You know, my favorite wild word
is not on the list," she said.

"It's standing right in front of me."

A gurgling sound was coming from a clearing,
light flickering on a glassy surface.
It was a small stream.
A BROOK.
Dancing, sparkling, singing,
it knew exactly where it was going.
Joyful thread of water, cutting through the trees.

"The last wild word is *you!*" Mimi said.
"You were named after this tiny stream
that your mother always cherished."

One could only imagine such a perfect name for

The Keeper of Wild Words.

"Mimi, I never told you what I needed help with," said Brook.
"What is it?" Mimi said.
"I need something special for show and tell tomorrow . . .
  and now I have it!"

The night sky would soon be painted,
stars gleaming overhead,
a beautiful wild curtain closing on the day.

Mimi's wild words were safe.
They were shared, and remembered.
Understood, deeply loved.

When the wild wraps around you

it stays forever in your heart.

AUTHOR'S NOTE

This book was inspired by an article I read that astounded me. The *Oxford Junior Dictionary* removed over 100 natural words from its pages. They no longer felt these words had relevance for today's children. They were replaced by words such as

Analog

Cautionary Tale

Chatroom

Conflict

Creep

Database

Drought

MP3 Player

Negotiate

Vandalism

Voicemail

At first I was angry,
then disillusioned, and ultimately
very sad. But the beauty of being a writer is
that you can create a world that you want to see.
I decided to write a book where some of these lost
wild words would be celebrated and recognized
beyond the pages of the dictionary. To perhaps shed
light on what is transpiring, by bringing them to life,
and have children and their parents be aware of how
much we need to sustain the language of the natural
world. I hope I've done that with this book. I hope
every one of us will be Keepers of Wild Words.
I cannot imagine a world without
these beautiful words in it.

With love,

Brooke